Ballet

Amy Hunter

Contents

Ballet Dancers

Ballet is a kind of dance.
Girls and boys can do ballet.

Girls are called **ballerinas**.

Boys are called dancers.

Ballet School

Ballet dancers go to ballet school.
They learn to dance.

Ballet dancers dance every day at school.
It is hard work.

It takes a long time to be
a good ballet dancer.

Five Ballet Steps

Ballet dancers learn to stand in five ways.

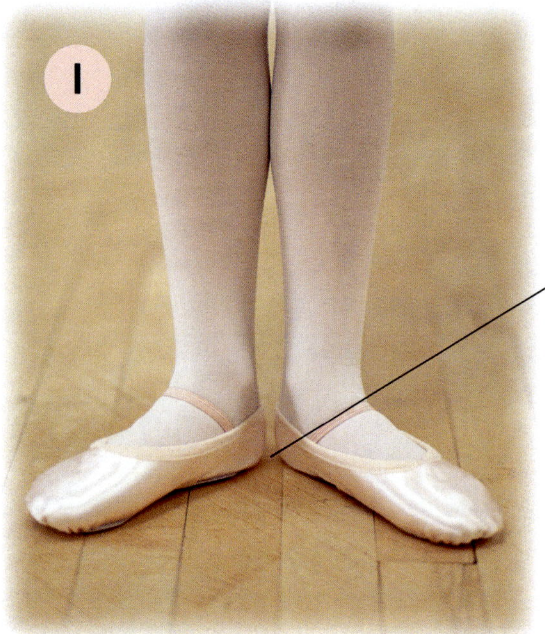

First Position
The heels are together.

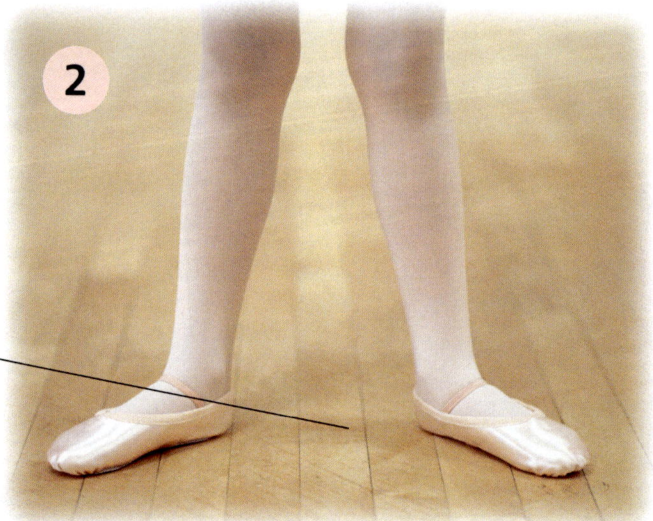

Second Position
The heels are not together.

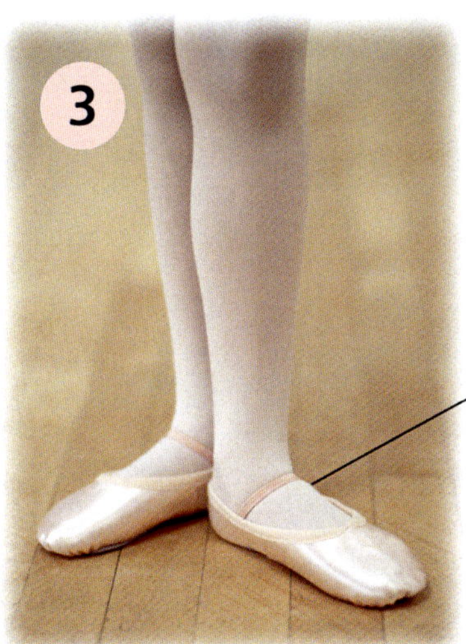

Third Position
This foot is in front of the other foot.

Fourth Position
This foot is more in front of the other foot.

Fifth Position
The toes and heels of the feet are touching.

Ballet dancers learn to jump.

Ballet dancers learn to turn around and around.

Girls learn to dance on their tip-toes.

Boys learn to lift up the girls.

Ballet Clothes

This ballerina wears
a short skirt.
It is called a **tutu**.
You can see her legs
as she dances.

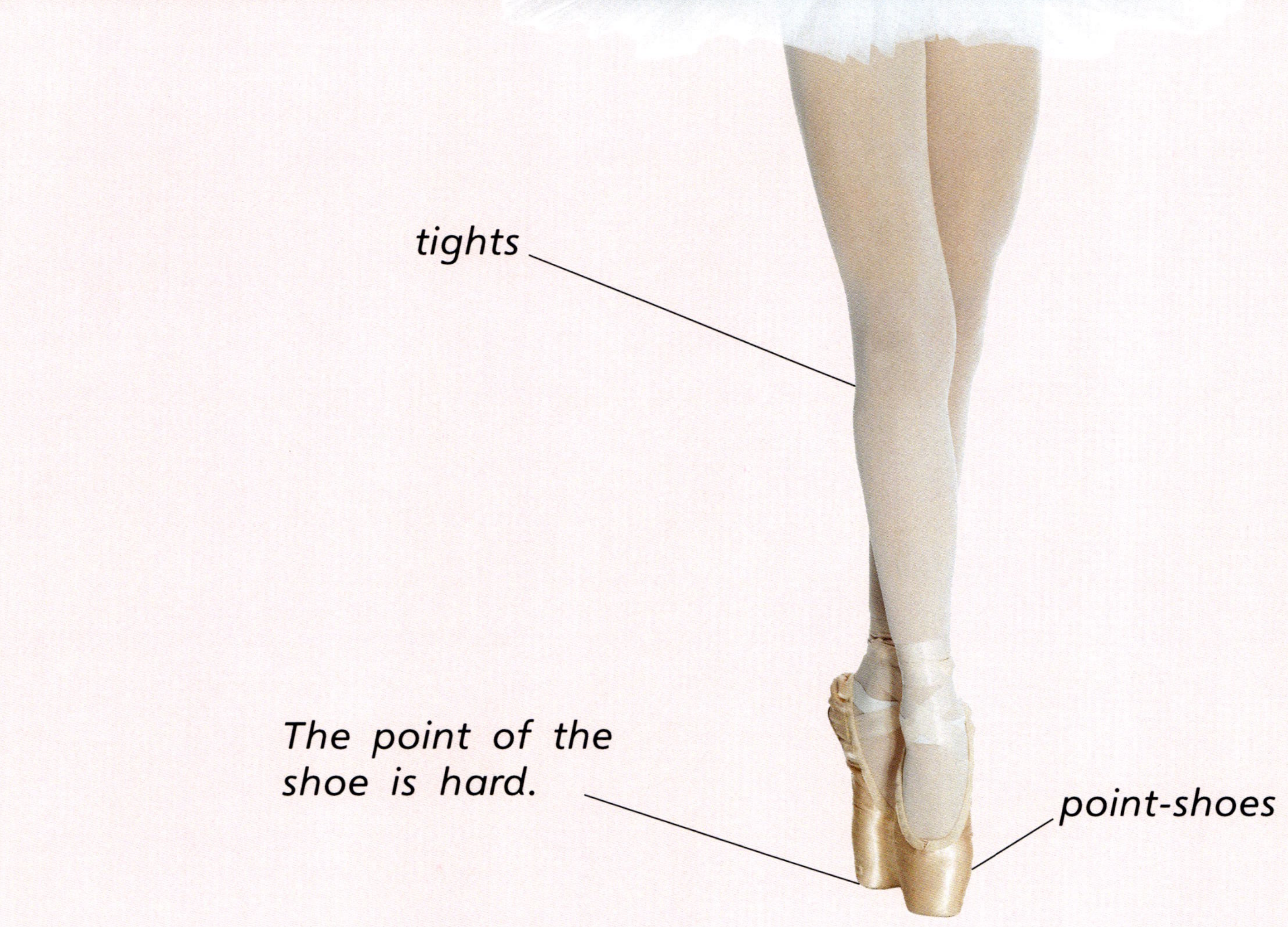

This ballerina wears ballet shoes.
They help her to dance on her toes.

On Stage

Ballet dancers dance on stage.

They put on make-up.
They put on **costumes**.

Ballet dancers tell a story when they dance.

This ballet tells a story about toys.
The toys come to life!

Glossary

ballerinas girls who do ballet

costumes clothes worn by dancers when they are on stage

tutu a kind of skirt that ballerinas wear